# The Velveteen Rabbit
## A Tale of Love

# The Velveteen Rabbit
## A Tale of Love

Illustrated by Elena Kucharik

Adapted by Jennifer Boudart

Publications International, Ltd.

On Christmas morning the boy just couldn't wait to go downstairs and see what Santa had brought him. The night before he could hardly sleep thinking about all of the wonderful presents he would receive. When the boy arrived downstairs, he couldn't believe his eyes! Normally his stocking was filled with candy, but this year it held a wonderful surprise: a velveteen rabbit.

The boy was filled with joy when he saw the velveteen rabbit. He kissed the rabbit and squeezed its soft, squishy tummy. The boy held his new friend under his arm while he opened all of his other gifts. That Christmas the boy received many new toys which joined his old toys in the nursery. With so many toys to choose from, the boy forgot about the velveteen rabbit for a time. But the velveteen rabbit did not forget how nice it felt to be held in the boy's arms.

The nursery was filled with many different sorts of toys. There was a shiny toy soldier who looked very serious and dignified, a bright sailboat that really floated, and a car that buzzed and moved. The velveteen rabbit felt plain next to these toys. He was nothing but fluff and stitches. Only a stuffed horse was shabbier. Though the horse was old and frayed, he was wise. "Flashy toys don't last," he said. "They break easily, and they don't have anything lovable inside. They will never be real."

"What does it mean to be real?" asked the velveteen rabbit. "Does it mean being new forever?"

"No," explained the horse. "You become real after someone loves you for a long time. By then you are old and tattered, but that's okay. When you are real, you are truly beautiful!"

That night the boy asked his nanny for the toy dog which he liked to hold while he slept. The nanny was not in the mood to look for the dog, so she handed him the velveteen rabbit. "Here you go," she said. "This rabbit will help you get to sleep just fine."

The boy instantly forgot about the toy dog. He took the velveteen rabbit and held him tightly next to his body. The stuffed rabbit fit the crook of the boy's arm much better than the dog, and the boy quickly and happily fell asleep.

The velveteen rabbit felt so good that he didn't mind being a bit squashed. In fact, he didn't even notice. The velveteen rabbit loved being hugged so closely while the boy slept. Of all the toys in the nursery, the velveteen rabbit felt like he was the most special.

From that night on, the velveteen rabbit looked forward to bedtime, when the boy would hug him as he fell asleep. They spent days together, too. The boy loved the velveteen rabbit so much that he took him everywhere he went. Sometimes they went on picnics or played in the garden. Other times the boy treated the velveteen rabbit to long rides in the wheelbarrow. No matter what they did, they always had a wonderful time.

The velveteen rabbit's heart was filled with joy. He truly loved the boy. He was so happy on the inside that he didn't even notice how shabby he was becoming on the outside. His fur was getting dirty from all the trips outdoors. And the space between his ears was beginning to wear thin from all the nights of being hugged and petted at bedtime.

One afternoon the boy left the velveteen
rabbit hiding in the garden while he went
to pick berries. Suddenly lightning flashed,
and rain began to pour. The boy became
frightened and ran straight home. Hours
later he realized the velveteen rabbit was
still outside. Who would rescue him?
Nanny, of course!

Grumbling, the nanny headed outside
with a flashlight and found the velveteen
rabbit. The nanny returned with a scowl
and said, "I can't believe I went out in the
rain to find your silly toy!"

The boy quickly snatched the velveteen
rabbit from her. "He is not a toy! He's
real!" he shouted.

The velveteen rabbit was cold. His fur
was dripping with water. But he didn't
mind at all. The boy said he was real! That
meant the boy loved him!

One day the boy placed the velveteen rabbit on a nice bed of leaves while he went off to play in the woods. Suddenly two strange creatures appeared. They looked like rabbits, but they had twitching noses and hopped by themselves.

They came closer to the velveteen rabbit and looked carefully at his slightly tattered fur. "Hello!" one said, twitching his nose. "Would you like to play with us? We're going to hop through the tall grass."

"N-no thank you," the velveteen rabbit stuttered. He did not want the strangers to know that he could not hop by himself like they could.

"He's not real," said the other rabbit to his friend. "He's just a toy!" The two, furry rabbits hopped away. The velveteen rabbit watched them disappear. How he wished he could follow them!

Soon the velveteen rabbit forgot all about the two rabbits he had met in the woods. He was too busy spending time with the boy. By now, the velveteen rabbit was more tattered than ever. His plush fur was dirty and torn, and he left trails of stuffing everywhere he went. He didn't seem to notice, though. He was happy with the boy. He didn't mind how he looked.

One day something awful happened. The boy became ill, and everything changed. While he was sick, the velveteen rabbit became very worried. He stayed close to the boy and did whatever he could to help him get better. He spent his days imagining all the fun they would have when the boy was well again. At night he whispered his plans to the boy. The velveteen rabbit was sure he could make him feel better.

With the velveteen rabbit's help, the boy soon got better. Things were wonderful again. The boy and the velveteen rabbit went to the garden and played and did all the fun things they used to do.

The velveteen rabbit was happier than he had ever been until the boy and his family went on vacation. The velveteen rabbit was accidentally left behind!

The velveteen rabbit watched the boy leave, and he began to cry. In the spot where his tears fell, a beautiful flower grew. The flower held a magical figure who said, "Hello, dear rabbit, your love for the boy has earned you the right to become real!"

"Wasn't I real already?" asked the rabbit.

"Only to the boy. Now, I will make you real to everyone!" Suddenly the rabbit could hop on his own.

When the boy returned home from his long vacation, he headed to the woods to play. As he was walking, the boy saw a rabbit who looked very familiar. His glossy fur coat had a dark patch over the left eye. The rabbit did not run away when he saw the boy. He hopped right up to him as if to say hello. "That's amazing," thought the boy. "This bunny looks just like my old friend, the velveteen rabbit."

The boy smiled as he thought of all the fun he had shared with the velveteen rabbit. He did not know that his friend had returned, a real rabbit at last, and was standing right in front of him!

Though he lived in the woods now with the other rabbits, and could move on his own, the rabbit would never forget the boy's love. The boy's love for him had helped to make him real.

# *One to Grow On*
## Love

In this story the velveteen rabbit learned all about love. He learned how good it feels to love and to be loved. The loving friendship that the boy and the velveteen rabbit shared made the rabbit feel great.

The velveteen rabbit also learned that love can change things. When the boy was feeling ill, the velveteen rabbit's love helped him get better.

The story of the velveteen rabbit reminds us how wonderful it is to have loved ones. No matter what, you know they will always care for you.

# The End